BEN 10 ALIEN FORCE™

THE COMPLETE GUIDE

by Tracey West
with Katherine Noll

SCHOLASTIC INC.

New York Toronto London Auckland Sydney
Mexico City New Delhi Hong Kong Buenos Aires

ISBN-13: 978-0-545-16049-0
ISBN-10: 0-545-16049-9

TM & © 2009 Cartoon Network.
(s09)

Published by Scholastic Inc.
SCHOLASTIC and associated logos are trademarks and/or registered trademarks of Scholastic Inc.

12 11 10 9 8 7 6 5 4 3 2 1   9 10 11 12 13 14/0

Printed in the U.S.A.
First printing, May 2009

CONTENTS

HOW IT ALL BEGAN

FIVE YEARS AGO . . .

A mysterious alien device crash-landed on Earth and was discovered by ten-year-old Ben Tennyson. The device, the Omnitrix, allowed Ben to transform into many different aliens, each with its own unique powers.

Once Ben put on the Omnitrix, he couldn't take it off. So he used his powers to become a superhero. With the help of his grandpa Max and cousin Gwen, he defeated Vilgax, a warlord intent on taking over Earth.

Sometime later, Ben found a way to remove the Omnitrix. The alien threat was over, and Ben wanted to have a normal life. But now . . .

Ben is fifteen years old, and his grandpa Max is missing. Together Ben and Gwen investigate his disappearance and discover that a new alien threat exists. Ben must strap on the Omnitrix once more.

This time, the alien forms he can access are different — and the planet is in much greater danger. . . .

BEN'S 10

When Ben first put on the Omnitrix, he discovered he could transform into ten different alien species. Each species had its own personality that melded with Ben's when he transformed.

It took Ben a while to grow accustomed to the abilities of his different alien forms. After he donned the Omnitrix again, he discovered that he couldn't access his original ten forms. Instead, he found ten new alien species were available to him.

Like before, each of the alien species has its own special powers and personality. It's up to Ben to decide which alien to use in any situation. Luckily, Ben is a quick thinker who usually makes the right choice. And if he's wrong, no problem! As long as he can reach his Omnitrix, Ben can choose another form.

BEN

When Ben uses the Omnitrix, his DNA binds with the alien DNA inside the watch. So whether he's a giant dinosaurlike alien or a crab creature with a giant brain, he's still Ben — a fifteen-year-old kid who likes monster movies, smoothies, and sumo wrestlers.

Before he picked up the Omnitrix again, Ben was enjoying normal teenage life — hanging out with his friends and playing on the soccer team. But it's hard to be normal when you're saving the world from evil aliens. Ben doesn't have any regrets. He knows what he's doing is important work, and he's proud to follow in the footsteps of his grandpa Max, an intergalactic police officer.

Still, it's not easy being a hero. Saving the universe

THE SECRET OF THE OMNITRIX

The Omnitrix was created by Azmuth, a scientist from the planet Galvan Prime. Azmuth's goal was to preserve the DNA of alien species around the universe. Azmuth finally revealed the Omnitrix's big secret to Ben: It contains the DNA of more than one million alien species!

Azmuth has safeguarded the Omnitrix so that Ben can only access some of the alien forms. Azmuth alone can remove the safeguards. Since it's nearly impossible to remove the Omnitrix from Ben, it looks like he'll be the guardian of these species for the rest of his life. That's a big job!

takes up a lot of study and hang-out time. And it's not easy keeping his secret. For a while, even his own parents didn't know their son could transform into alien beings.

The Omnitrix might just be the most powerful device in the universe. So what's it doing strapped to the wrist of a teenage earthling? The answer lies in Ben's heart. Many people would try to use the Omnitrix to gain power for themselves, but Ben would never do that. And even though he can cause massive destruction in some of his forms, he prefers to find a peaceful solution to a problem whenever possible.

Will Ben ever get to have a normal life? Maybe not. But after all the amazing adventures he's had, maybe being normal is not such a big deal.

ALIEN X

Alien X is Ben's most powerful form — and one he rarely uses.

Alien X looks like a field of stars in humanoid form. Ben transformed into Alien X to stop a broken dam from washing away an entire valley. With one motion, Alien X sent the water rolling backward, and the dam was repaired.

When Ben transformed, he found himself floating in a star-filled void. He faced two giant, glowing green faces and learned they were the two most powerful beings in the universe. Serena is the voice of love and compassion. Belicus is the voice of rage and aggression. They haven't been able to agree on anything for millions and millions of years. But they both agreed to keep Ben trapped with them forever. Finally, they'd found someone who could break a tie!

When Ben is floating inside Alien X, the alien is frozen, like a statue. He can't move or act unless Serena and Belicus agree. Ben begged the two beings to use Alien X to help save Earth, but they wouldn't. However, they finally did agree to allow Ben to transform into another form.

Ben knows he got lucky. The next time he transforms into Alien X, he risks being stuck with Serena and Belicus for the rest of eternity.

ALIEN X'S HOME WORLD

Alien X belongs to a species known as Celestialsapiens. They live in a place called Zvezda. It's not a planet, but a collection of gases and energy. The species survives in this murky atmosphere by becoming one with the stars.

BIG CHILL

Ben might be a typical fifteen-year-old, but when he transforms into Big Chill he turns into a creature that looks like it came straight out of a nightmare! Big Chill has a spooky voice to match his specterlike appearance. It's hard not to chill out when Big Chill is around. His breath can make his enemies' temperatures drop below zero. *Brrr!*

It's no wonder Big Chill can use the cold as a weapon. The planet he comes from, Kylmyys, is completely covered by ice and snow. It's always winter there. Big Chill's species, the Necrofriggian, are the only beings that can live on this inhospitable planet. That's because they don't have bodies, so there's nothing to freeze. The Necrofriggian are mere mists, able to float through solid matter. And if one passes through you, you'll be frozen into unconsciousness.

BIG MOMMA?

Big Chill has done some amazing things during a fight. He's become intangible, allowing attacks to pass right through him. He's disabled hundreds of alien guards just by freezing them. But Ben began to wonder if he was losing control of Big Chill — and the Omnitrix — when the alien began consuming vast quantities of metal. Everyone was worried — until they followed Big Chill to an empty field outside of town. It turned out he was making a giant metal dome. Kevin smashed it and tiny baby Necrofriggians flew out! Big Chill needed the extra metal to create an incubator for the little Chills.

BRAIN STORM

Ben was trying to transform into Jet Ray when he became Brain Storm for the first time. When he first saw his crablike body, he exclaimed, "I'm not Jet Ray. I'm a seafood platter!"

Brain Storm has sharp pincers and a hard exoskeleton that covers up his massive brain. This brain makes Brain Storm a supersmart problem solver, but his species has a handy attack power too. Brain Storm can open his shell to reveal his brain and zap his opponents with highly charged lightning bolts. He calls this attack an "electroencephalitic mind blast."

This brilliant alien is a Cerebrocrustacean from the planet Encephalonus IV. The skies above this planet are continually torn apart by never-ending electrical storms. These storms are the main source of power for the planet. The inhabitants of Encephalonus I, II, and III depleted the energy on their planets, so the Cerebrocrustaceans of Encephalonus IV evolved to create electrical storms using only the power of their minds.

BATTLE OF THE BRAINS

Who is smarter, Azmuth or Brain Storm? It depends on whom you ask. When the HighBreed were about to launch their invasion of Earth, Azmuth and Brain Storm needed to fly an Antarian Obliterator warship to stop them. Azmuth and Brain Storm argued over who would pilot the ship.

"With my oversized cranium and the intellectual superiority that naturally follows from it, I am obviously the correct form to pilot this vehicle under these trying conditions," Brain Storm said.

"Are you implying that you're smarter than me because your head is bigger?" asked an insulted Azmuth.

"No. I'm implying that I'm smarter than you because my *brain* is bigger," Brain Storm replied.

Either way, they're both geniuses. Too bad Brain Storm can't take Ben's physics tests for him!

CHROMASTONE

ChromaStone is a Crystalsapien — a living crystal. That means that ChromaStone is practically indestructible. Laser beams shot from alien weapons don't damage ChromaStone at all. And while radiation is dangerous to most living creatures, this species can absorb it and transform it into light — anything from a laser blast to a soft glow to light a darkened pathway.

The Crystalsapien species is native to the planet MorOtesi. Their world was once lush and green, but after the ozone layer decayed millions of years ago, it became barren and rocky. The planet's original inhabitants couldn't handle being exposed to constant electromagnetic radiation. They died out. But the Crystalsapiens evolved to thrive on that radiation and develop a complex society on MorOtesi.

CHROMASTONE TAKES ON THE BULLIES

JT and Cash are bullies that Ben has had to face since the second grade. But they were never truly a danger until they stole an alien robot arm from Kevin's car. Cash put the arm on and was possessed by Techadon, a powerful robot assassin. He went looking for Ben to settle the score between them, but he had to face ChromaStone instead!

Cash's massive energy blast attacks bounced harmlessly off the crystalline ChromaStone. When Cash tried another attack, ChromaStone absorbed the blast and discharged it right back at Cash, knocking him over. Cash had to give up battling with ChromaStone and instead fight the alien technology that was taking over his body. He succeeded—and ended up with a new respect for Ben.

ECHO ECHO

What's better than being able to turn into ten different alien forms? How about changing into as many as you need in one shot, all with a smack of the Omnitrix? Echo Echo might be small, but he has the unique ability to make endless duplicates of himself. What he lacks in size he more than makes up for in quantity!

Echo Echo comes from Sonorosia, a planet known for its massive gorges and immense canyons. They make Earth's Grand Canyon look like a pinhole. All those caverns make for a great place to generate echoes and manipulate sound, and that's where Echo Echo draws his powers from. Even his lowest-powered sonic wave blasts can knock out opponents. At full force, they can shatter steel. If you spot an army of Echo Echoes headed your way, grab some earplugs!

ECHO ECHO VS. ARGIT

Dodging sleeping quills shot from Argit, a porcupinelike alien, is no easy feat. But when Argit stole the Rustbucket II, Grandpa Max's motor home, Ben and Gwen were willing to do anything to get it back. And Echo Echo was the perfect alien form to help. Even though quills were flying everywhere, they couldn't hit every Echo Echo. A single Echo Echo remained, and he quickly multiplied into a line of little aliens determined to face down the barrage of quills.

All the Echo Echoes generated one huge reverb blast that slammed the quills backward — right into a very surprised Argit, who immediately fell asleep. When he came to, he tried to shoot his quills again. But Echo Echo had taken care of that. The little aliens had superglued them to Argit's head!

GOOP

Able to polymorph into any shape, Goop is Ben's most versatile form. But Gwen and Kevin aren't big fans of Goop. He really grosses them out! That's because Goop is a two-hundred-pound ball of green slime. Besides being able to change shape at will, Goop can also shoot out a powerful acid that he secretes from his body.

Goop may look gross, but he fits right in on his home world, Viscosia. The piping-hot planet is home to volcanoes flowing with molten lava. Goop is a Polymorph, and when his species mysteriously lost their native home, scientists moved them to Viscosia. It was a perfect match.

GOOP VS. TECHADON

Ben first transformed into Goop when he was fighting a Techadon robot. No attacks seemed to bother this robot, so Ben decided to take it down from the inside. He became Goop and slipped inside the robot. Goop expanded, causing the robot to explode from within.

Of course, that meant Goop exploded too. Gobs of slimy stuff landed on Gwen and Kevin. Goop quickly put himself back together and transformed back into Ben. Goop may be messy, but he cleans up pretty quickly!

HUMUNGOUSAUR

"Guess what time it is?" Humungousaur once asked a group of alien enemies. "It's hero time!"

It's no wonder Ben feels like a superhero when he's Humungousaur. It's Ben's most physically powerful alien form. He can pick up a highway overpass in one hand or smash a house with ease. This dinosaurlike alien is all about brute strength. But that doesn't mean he can't take his opponents by surprise. Humungousaur is a size changer who can reach nearly sixty feet tall, astounding his adversaries and taking the battle to a whole new level.

On your next vacation you might be tempted to go to Terradino, Humungousaur's home world and the place where his species, the Vaxasaurian, live. Terradino boasts perfect weather and beautiful scenery. It looks like a tropical paradise. But Terradino is home to many species, not just the Vaxasaurians. These different alien species are constantly at war, fighting for control of the planet. Because of their amazing strength, the Vaxasaurians have been able to restore order temporarily. But there are still worries that the violence and chaos will return, destroying this beautiful planet once and for all.

HUMUNGOUSAUR SAVES THE DAY

When an out-of-control eighteen-wheeler truck went sliding off an overpass, crashing onto the support beams and causing them to crumble, Ben knew exactly the alien form he'd need to get this job done. Humungousaur was the only one strong enough to hoist the overpass onto his massive shoulders, giving Gwen the chance to create an energy ramp so the drivers stranded on the buckling overpass could slide to safety. Once everyone was okay, he had to deal with another problem: The truck that caused the accident had caught fire. But Humungousaur isn't all muscles and no brains. He laid the concrete overpass on top of the fire to extinguish it. Now that's a real hero!

JET RAY

If Ben needs to get some-where fast, Jet Ray is the way to go! This manta-ray-like alien can swim through water or fly through the air. In fact, Jet Ray can fly at several times the speed of sound. But swiftness isn't Jet Ray's only skill. He can maneuver eas-ily as he flies at top speeds, avoiding obstacles and dodg-ing attacks.

Jet Ray is an Aerophib-ian, a unique species that can survive both in the air and in the water. That's because the Aerophibian home world, the planet Aeropela, is completely covered in water. There is not a spot of dry land to be found. Most species there exist either under the sea or in the sky.

If you can't fly and don't know how to swim, Aeropela is probably not a planet you'd like to visit. The weather isn't very nice. This watery world is plagued by fog, rain, and rag-ing hurricanes.

JET RAY VS. VERDONA

The ultrafast, ultramaneuverable Jet Ray has helped Ben out of many tight spots. But Ben never could have imagined that as Jet Ray he'd battle his own grandmother! When a mysterious woman blasted Ben, Gwen, and Kevin with glowing energy, Ben transformed into Jet Ray and chased after her. Although Jet Ray had no trouble keeping up with her, catching her was a different story. She dodged his whip cracks and effortlessly evaded his neuro-blasts.

When Jet Ray finally pinned her down with his sting-er, she formed an energy sphere around it. Who could be strong enough to defeat Jet Ray? It turns out the mystery woman was Verdona, Ben and Gwen's grandmother and a powerful Anodite alien!

SPIDERMONKEY

Spidermonkey looks like a monkey with four arms, with the same amazing agility as its earthly equivalent. Like a spider, he can stick to walls, and he can even spin webs as strong as steel cables. These powers make Spidermonkey a hero to be reckoned with. When Ben transforms into this alien form, there's no monkeying around!

Spidermonkey is a member of the Arachna-Paniscus species. They live in the rain forests of the planet Arachna, a tropical paradise. Unfortunately, the other inhabitants of this planet think Arachna-Paniscus are delicious, so this species must live in the high treetops, spinning webs to make shelter. Because they're always hunted, they're constantly on the move.

SPIDERMONKEY VS. THE DNALIENS

The DNAliens often attack Ben and his friends in large groups. When it was time for close combat with these slime-spewing creatures, Ben found that turning into Spidermonkey was his best bet.

A truckload of DNAliens once ambushed Ben, Gwen, and Kevin on the road. Ben transformed into Spidermonkey and used each of his four arms to toss the DNAliens aside. They fired their laser beams at him, but Spidermonkey easily dodged them. Then he blasted the aliens with his own sticky web goo, causing them to drop their laser guns. Even then, the DNAliens didn't give up. They lunged at Spidermonkey, but he deflected them with some monkey martial arts moves. The DNAliens scattered, and Ben and his friends were safe.

SWAMPFIRE

"Ew. What's that's smell?" Ben asked the first time he transformed into the muck-encrusted Swampfire. "Is that me?"

So maybe Swampfire does stink. But you would too if you came from Methanos, a steaming swamp of a planet. Between the horrible stench, the toxic atmosphere, and the sudden bursts of methane gas that shoot geysers of flame into the air, it's not exactly the most welcoming of worlds. But the Methanosians, the species that live there, can handle it.

Swampfire may look like a walking compost heap, but thanks to the large amounts of highly flammable methane gas his body produces, he's able to shoot fire from his hands like a flamethrower. Ammunition passes right through his muddy body without harm. If an attack is serious enough to sever a limb, all Swampfire has to do is pick up the body part, stick it back where it belongs, and new roots will grow from his body, reattaching it.

SWAMPFIRE VS. THE ALIEN SWARM

When Ben strapped on the Omnitrix again, Swampfire was the first alien form he changed into. Since then, Swampfire has helped Ben out many times, but he really saved the day when Ben was trapped with a HighBreed on the desert planet Turrawuste. Thousands of tiny armadillolike aliens called Dasypodidae swarmed over Ben, burying him. Ben was able to activate the Omnitrix and transform. Swampfire cut a fiery swath through the throng of aliens, allowing him and the HighBreed to flee. The Dasypodidae pursued them, but Swampfire blasted a rocky overhang, causing a rock slide that buried the entire swarm of aliens.

BEN'S TEAM

Ben might wield the Omnitrix with all of its secret powers, but there's no way he could fight the alien threat by himself. When he was ten, Grandpa Max guided Ben and Gwen on their alien-fighting missions. With Grandpa Max missing, Ben and Gwen were left to battle on their own.

But they weren't alone for long. Their old nemesis, Kevin Levin, joined their quest. Every time they faced danger, a new friend popped up to help them out. Ben soon learned that no matter how powerful his alien forms were, he wouldn't be able to accomplish anything without his friends.

In this section, you'll meet characters who are all good guys at heart. Some of them are alien, some are human, and some are members of Ben's family. To-gether, they make a terrific team.

GWEN TENNYSON

Ben's cousin Gwen doesn't use a special device to transform into an alien. She doesn't need to. Thanks to her grandmother, Gwen is half alien herself, and she has some pretty awesome powers to prove it.

When she was ten years old, Gwen discovered she had the ability to use magical charms and talismans. (Gwen didn't realize she had alien DNA until she was fifteen.) Knowing this power could help her family keep Earth safe from aliens,

GWEN AND KEVIN

Gwen may be able to keep her cool when she's fighting off a horde of DNAliens, but there is one creature in the universe that really gets under her skin: Kevin Levin.

Something always seems to stand in the way of Gwen and Kevin becoming girlfriend and boyfriend. They tried to go to a school dance together once but got derailed when they had to stop Big Chill from going on a rampage. When they're not fighting aliens, Kevin is hesitant to ask Gwen out. Gwen can't figure him out. She knows he likes her — so what's he waiting for?

Gwen's not sure if she'll ever figure out Kevin, but that's okay with her. Whatever happens, she knows he'll always be a good friend.

Gwen practiced and studied for years. As a result, Gwen is now able to produce powerful energy blasts. She can create a strong shield capable of withstanding serious attacks, or use her energy to take down enemies.

But Gwen's power doesn't come from magic — it comes from her alien heritage. Gwen is part Anodite. These aliens from the planet Anodyne grow to become beings of pure energy. If Gwen chooses, she can go to Anodyne, shed her human body, and live as an Anodite. But Gwen likes being human too much to give up that part of herself.

Even without her alien powers, Gwen has all the qualities of a great hero. She's a martial arts master, she keeps cool under pressure, and she's got a logical mind that makes her a great strategist.

KEVIN E. LEVIN

Kevin used to be a villain intent on taking over the world with his superpowers. So what is he doing helping Ben and Gwen?

It started when Kevin got out of the Null Void, where he did time for his crimes. He didn't exactly reform right away. First he started dealing in illegal alien tech. Then Ben and Gwen and a Plumber named Magister Labrid caught him dealing dangerous Level 5 technology to the Forever Knights. The knights got away, and Kevin agreed to help track them down.

Kevin helped destroy the knights' weapons, but Magister Labrid died during the battle. When that happened, Kevin took his Plumber's Badge and agreed to help Ben and Gwen fight the alien threat. His feelings for Gwen were definitely part of the reason for his change of heart. And Ben and Gwen later learned that Kevin's real dad was a Plumber, just like Grandpa Max. His dad passed his powers to Kevin, and deep down, Kevin wants to be just like his dad.

Those powers are pretty cool. If Kevin absorbs a solid substance, his body can turn into that substance. He needs to touch something big, though, or only his hand will transform.

Kevin's favorite forms are stone and metal. They make him nearly impervious to laser attacks and give him super-strength. Once, Kevin touched a rubber tire and bounced around, knocking down bad guys.

Kevin's still pretty tough, and he's got a fiery temper and a sometimes reckless sense of adventure. Qualities like these can be useful when you're fighting aliens — as long as they're under control. In fact, Ben and Gwen's grandmother, Verdona, said that Kevin reminded her of a young Grandpa Max.

KEVIN'S WHEELS

Ben and Gwen aren't old enough to drive, so Kevin takes the alien fighters everywhere in his restored 1970s green-and-black muscle car. The car is Kevin's pride and joy, and he spends hours every day taking care of it.

Fighting aliens can take a toll on your vehicle, and the car has been smashed, dented, crashed, and blown up several times. Once, time-traveling hero Paradox turned Kevin's car back in time so it was brand-new. Naturally, it got busted up again a short time later. That didn't stop Kevin. He's loyal to his car, no matter what happens to it. He spends what little free time he has adding bits and pieces of alien technology to the car.

GRANDPA MAX

Grandpa Max is Ben and Gwen's fun-loving, kindhearted grandfather. When Ben first strapped on the Omnitrix, Grandpa Max stepped in to help. He knew a little something about the world of aliens. After all, Grandpa Max is a Plumber, an intergalactic police officer.

After Ben, Gwen, and Grandpa Max defeated Vilgax, things on Earth were peaceful for five years. Then Ben went to visit Grandpa Max in his motor home, the Rustbucket II, and found a DNAlien there instead. But Grandpa Max had left behind a mysterious message. He warned Ben that there was renewed alien activity on Earth.

Ben knew there was only one thing to do: Put the Omnitrix back on. Together with Gwen and Kevin, he began to search for Grandpa Max. Kevin located another message from Max in which he told Ben to find as many Plumbers' kids as he could to fight the alien invasion. Ben was worried, but at least they were getting closer to Grandpa Max.

A short time later, Ben and Gwen found Grandpa Max.

THE RUSTBUCKET II

When Grandpa Max's first motor home, the Rustbucket, was destroyed, he went out and bought a new one. The Rustbucket II used to be loaded with alien technology, but a tech runner  named Argit stole it. He almost got the Rustbucket II as well, but Ben and Gwen stopped him.

He'd been captured by High-Breed aliens after he discovered their DNAlien-making factory. Ben, Gwen, and Kevin came to the rescue, but they were surrounded by a horde of DNAliens. There was no way out.

That's when Grandpa Max made the ultimate sacrifice. He turned his Null Void Projector into a makeshift grenade and blew the factory to pieces. Grandpa Max was lost in the explosion, and Ben and Gwen thought he was dead. Luckily, Max had transported into the Null Void, where he became the hero "the Wrench" and saved the Null Void from a villain named D'Void.

After fixing the Null Void, Grandpa Max returned to Earth so he could train the Plumbers' kids to be skilled Plumbers. As for Ben, he was just glad to have his grandfather back home at last.

THE PLUMBERS

On Earth, the Plumbers are a secret government organization charged with protecting the planet from alien and paranormal threats. There are Plumbers on every planet. Together, they form an intergalactic police force that keeps peace in the universe.

Plumbers have ranks, just like a police force. Since there are millions of planets in the universe, a Plumber is usually in charge of a sector of space. This could include a few or maybe hundreds of planets.

Some alien Plumbers have lived on Earth, disguised as humans. When the HighBreed attacked, Ben sought out the children of the Plumbers to help him fight them. The Plumbers' kids include Kevin Levin, Alan Albright, Mike Morningstar, and Manny, Helen, and Pierce.

Plumbers have cool tools that they use to combat bad guys. When a criminal is captured, a Plumber uses glowing blue energy cuffs to immobilize his wrists. One zap from a Plumber's Null Void Projector can send a criminal into the Null Void forever. And every Plumber wears a round badge that contains a holographic map showing the location of other Plumbers.

The Plumbers do a great job of keeping the universe safe, but sometimes there are just too many bad guys and not enough Plumbers. That's where Ben and his friends come in.

JULIE YAMAMOTO

When you're saving the world from aliens, it's hard to find time to do normal teenage stuff. So Ben lucked out when he met Julie, who thinks monsters and aliens are as cool as her favorite sport, tennis.

That's a good thing, because when Ben and Julie went on their first date, they were attacked by carnival rides that came to life and kidnapped Julie. Ben, Gwen, and Kevin soon discovered the rides were actually a creature called Ship, an alien that can transform into mechanical devices. Ship was just trying to get Ben's attention so he could help the pilot of a crashed spaceship.

Julie ended up unofficially adopting Ship. She uses Ship to help Ben and the others fight dangerous aliens. When she's not busy helping to save the world, she likes watching monster movies with Ben and shopping with Gwen.

VERDONA

Verdona is Ben and Gwen's grandmother. She may look like a sweet lady with white hair, but that's not her true form. She's really an Anodite alien from the planet Anodyne — a being of pure energy. Anodites are free spirits who can master the manipulation of Manna, life energy.

When Verdona was younger, she fell in love with Max Tennyson and settled down. She's the mother of Ben's dad, Karl, and Gwen's dad, Mike. But she left her Earth family behind long ago to explore her heritage on Anodyne.

Every once in a while, Verdona checks in to see what's happening on Earth. When she discovered that Gwen had inherited her abilities, she wanted Gwen to go back to Anodyne with her, leaving her human body behind. Gwen wanted to stay on Earth, but Verdona wouldn't take no for an answer. Spidermonkey and Kevin battled Verdona until she changed her mind. She left Earth peacefully, but promised to drop in again to see how Gwen was doing.

SANDRA AND KARL TENNYSON

Ben's parents are an easygoing couple who love nature. But when they discovered that their son had been fighting aliens for years without their knowledge, they got tough.

Ben was grounded from saving the world — no cell phone, no computer, and above all, no using the Omnitrix. Sandra was especially worried about Ben's safety. And Karl never liked the secret life led by his father, Max. He didn't want Ben keeping secrets, either.

Then Kevin was locked in a losing battle with a High-Breed, and Ben had to make a tough choice between obeying his parents and saving his friend. Ben chose to save Kevin, and Sandra and Karl realized that what Ben was doing was important. Now they let Ben fight the alien menace whenever he wants — as long as he's home at a reasonable hour and remembers to wear a jacket when it's chilly out.

KEN TENNYSON

Gwen and Ben always looked up to Gwen's older brother, Ken. Ken took Ben to his first soccer game. He snuck Gwen and her friends backstage when his band played. Ken was a typical college student with a junky car and a pretty normal life. He had no idea his little sister and cousin were fighting evil aliens.

Then Ken's car broke down in the wrong part of town one day. DNAliens captured him and used him as bait to lure Grandpa Max to their hideout. They used a parasite called a Xenocite to turn Ken into a hideous DNAlien.

With the help of Ben, Gwen, and Kevin, Grandpa Max rescued Ken. Ben used the Omnitrix to transform Ken into a human again. Now Ken knows his family's secret — as well as the secret threat that could destroy all of humankind.

ALAN ALBRIGHT

When Ben first used the Omnitrix, he was able to transform into Heatblast, a Pyronite alien. Pyronites live on a star, Pyrus, instead of a planet. They're basically made of fire, able to shoot fireballs at will and absorb heat and flames.

So Ben was surprised to meet twelve-year-old Alan, who can transform into a Pyronite at will. Alan's dad was a Pyronite Plumber who gave his badge to Alan. At first, the police in Alan's small farming town were sure he was causing trouble, setting fires everywhere. Thanks to Ben's help, Alan proved the DNAliens were behind it all.

Ben asked Alan to join his team of alien fighters. Alan decided to stick close to home and help the sheriff fight off the alien threat there. But Ben knows that if he's in trouble, he can count on the new Heatblast to watch his back.

COOPER

Cooper is a shy, quiet kid who rarely leaves his basement computer lab. But Cooper doesn't spend all of his time on massively multiplayer online role-playing games. He's got a special talent. He's a technopath, which means he can communicate with and understand technology — including alien technology.

That's exactly why the HighBreed aliens want Cooper. They sent DNAliens to capture Cooper. Then they forced him to create their secret alien technology. Cooper didn't know exactly what he was making, but he was pretty sure it was going to be used for sinister purposes.

Ben, Gwen, and Kevin saved Cooper from the aliens, but they can't save him from the huge crush he has on Gwen. His yen for Gwen is one big reason he's sure to help Ben and his friends save the world if he's ever needed again.

SHIP

Ship is a Mechomorph from the moon Galvan B. Like the rest of his kind, Ship's body is made up entirely of living nanotechnology. That means he can absorb any technology and transform into it.

Most Mechomorphs are humanoid, but Ship is more like a pet. He came to Earth in the body of a Mechomorph space pilot. When the pilot's ship crashed, he sent out a part of his body — Ship — to get help. Ship sought out Ben, who was on a date with Julie at the time. Humungousaur saved the ship, and the pilot flew back home, leaving Ship behind. Since then, Ship has remained fond of Julie, and he visits her from time to time.

Ship once got into trouble when the Forever Knights kidnapped him and turned him into an Antarian Obliterator, a spaceship with awesome powers of destruction. Kevin and his friends helped Ship escape — and now Ship can transform into the gunship whenever he wants to.

MAGISTER LABRID

Magister Labrid was a Plumber who was working with Grandpa Max on a case before Max went missing. Labrid was an Aquarian, a fishlike alien. He wore a special suit that circulated water instead of air to keep him alive in Earth's atmosphere.

Labrid enlisted the help of Ben, Gwen, and Kevin to stop the Forever Knights from distributing a dangerous Level 5 weapon on Earth. He was gravely injured during a fierce battle with the knights and their guardian dragon.

Before he died, Labrid told Ben to keep investigating the alien invasion. Grandpa Max — and the people of Earth — were depending on it. Kevin took the Plumber's badge from Labrid's suit, vowing to help Ben and Gwen with their quest.

MAGISTER PRIOR GILHIL

Gilhil is a busy officer with more than three hundred planets under his charge. He's a big fan of law and order, and he really hates rule-breakers. When he got a tip that Ben, Gwen, and Kevin were "impersonating" Plumbers, he traveled to Earth to put them all under arrest.

Magister Gilhil took away Kevin's Plumber's badge and left the friends with a stern warning to stop impersonating officers of the law. He wasn't gone for long when a HighBreed attacked, forcing Ben, Gwen, and Kevin to use their powers to defend themselves. Gilhil arrived on the scene, ready to send them all to the Null Void for harming a "defenseless" HighBreed.

When the truth came out — that villain Darkstar was trying to frame his enemies — Gilhil realized that Ben and his friends were doing important work. Instead of arresting them, he drafted them as Plumbers in the quadrant.

AZMUTH

A zmuth is a Galvan scientist from the planet Galvan Prime. Galvans have superior intellect, and Azmuth just might be the smartest of them all: He is the inventor of the Omnitrix.

Azmuth created the device as a means to preserve the DNA of more than a million species in the universe. Fearing the Omnitrix would fall into the wrong hands, he sent it to Earth, where it ended up on the wrist of Ben Tennyson.

For the most part, Azmuth is happy that Ben is in control of his amazing device. But sometimes he's not so sure. He is slow to share all the secrets of the Omnitrix with Ben. However, when Earth was in danger of being destroyed by the HighBreed, Azmuth revealed some of the Omnitrix's greatest powers.

TYLER

Tyler, a twenty-six-year-old bass guitar player, was a pretty typical human living on planet Earth. Then he was captured, had a Xenocite strapped to his face, and had his DNA reprogrammed. Tyler became a DNAlien, a terrifying creature created by the HighBreed aliens to do their dirty work.

But Tyler resisted his reprogramming. When his commanders sent him on an important mission, Tyler rebelled. His human personality took over, although his memory was a little messed up.

Ben, Gwen, and Kevin rescued Tyler from the DNAliens pursuing him. Tyler was horrified when he realized he had been turned into a monster. But Ben used the Omnitrix to repair the damage done to Tyler's DNA. Now Tyler is one hundred percent human — and one of only a few people who know about the alien threat to Earth.

PARADOX

This Earth scientist can't remember his real name. Why? The last time he heard it was more than a hundred thousand years ago.

His adventure started in the 1950s, when he invented a chronolaugher — a subatomic drill designed to bore a tunnel into the fabric of space-time. When he tested the machine for the first time, a lab accident caused the time tunnel to malfunction. Paradox was trapped in the Event Horizon for eons. He didn't eat or sleep — he simply existed in a state suspended in time and space.

At first, Paradox went mad. Then he got smart. During his time in the Event Horizon, he became a master of time and space. Now he can freely travel to any place or time whenever he wants to. Paradox knows what's going to happen in the future and whether Ben and his friends will succeed or fail.

LU

Lu looks like a typical repairman you'd find in any town on Earth. And though he is a repairman, he's not very typical. Lu's an alien, and he works on Earth's moon.

The moon is home to a secret intergalactic communications center powered by a large crystal. If Earth is ever in trouble, the comm center can send a message of distress to other planets.

Keeping that comm center working at all times is Lu's job. It's a lonely life, with only robots to keep him company, but at least Lu knows he's doing important work. Ben found that out when a thief named Simian tricked Ben into helping him steal the crystal.

MANNY, HELEN, AND PIERCE

Manny and Helen realized the error of their ways after they tried to take down Ben, Gwen, and Kevin. They traveled into the Null Void to return everyone they had sent there by mistake. Inside, they discovered Pierce and Grandpa Max, who were working to save the Null Void from destruction. They all made it out in time to help Ben and the others save Earth from a HighBreed invasion.

These three young heroes are Plumbers' Helpers. They're half alien, half human, but unlike Ben or Alan, they are in their alien forms all the time. Manny is a Tretamand, Helen is a Kenceleran, and Pierce is an unknown species that can shoot quills like a porcupine.

When they first discovered their alien powers, Manny, Helen, and Pierce went on an alien-hunting spree. They sent any aliens they encountered into the Null Void without bothering to learn if they were good or bad. Pierce landed in the Null Void himself as a result.

REINRASSIG III

Okay, so this HighBreed alien and Ben aren't exactly *friends*. But they came as close as a High-Breed and a human ever will.

The relationship started on Earth, as Ben fought the High-Breed in his Echo Echo form. When the HighBreed tried to escape in his teleporter pod, Kevin damaged the transmission field. The malfunctioning teleporter sent both the HighBreed and Echo Echo to the planet Turrawuste, where Ben and his alien enemy were forced to work together to defend themselves against the planet's predatory monsters. Ben learned that the High-Breed's name was Reinrassig III, seventh son of the noble HighBreed House of DiRazza. Ben decided to call him "Reiny" for short.

Reiny refused to admit he could have a friendship with Ben, whom he considered to

be a revolting, genetically inferior creature. Then Reiny saved Ben's life, and Ben returned the favor. Even so, Reiny refused to leave the planet with Ben. Because he'd failed the HighBreed race, he exiled himself on the dangerous planet forever.

TINY

When Ben, Gwen, and Kevin first encountered this scary-looking monster, they thought it was an alien bent on destroying Earth. But poor Tiny was just a tiny baby, separated from her parents.

Back in 1952, Tiny and her parents were traveling to Alpha Promixa to colonize the planet. They were safely tucked into stasis pods for the long journey. Inside the pods, they could stay alive in a sleeplike state for years without food or water.

But the ship crash-landed on Earth and buried itself inside the ground. The alien family stayed in stasis for years until some DNAliens accidentally unearthed them. Tiny's stasis pod broke, and the DNAliens almost got hold of her. But Ben, Gwen, and Kevin reunited her with her family. Tiny became fond of her new friends, especially Gwen, whom she sees as a being of pure, glowing energy.

BAD GUYS

Earth is a crowded planet with lots of people, lots of natural resources, and lots of ways to get in trouble. For an alien bad guy, it's a planet that's ripe for the picking.

Some villains think big: They either want to dominate Earth or destroy it. Others are happy to fly under the radar, dealing in illegal weapons or stealing enough stuff to get by. Then there's another group of bad guys with one goal: to get revenge on Ben Tennyson.

No matter what the bad guys are after, Ben, Gwen, and Kevin will do whatever it takes to defeat them. Sometimes it's easy. Other times, it takes every bit of energy they've got. But what every villain quickly learns is that Ben and his friends don't give up.

THE FOREVER KNIGHTS

The men in this secret organization dress like knights in armor and live in castles. They seem to have an endless appetite for alien technology. They'll do whatever it takes to get it, no matter who gets hurt.

Ben learned that the knights have been around for a thousand years. Their order began when a group of knights captured a dragon. For centuries, generations of knights kept watch over the dragon. In their search for alien technology, they hoped to find a weapon strong enough to destroy the beast.

The knights didn't know it, but the creature they'd captured wasn't a dragon. Their

SOME KNIGHTS TO REMEMBER

CONNOR: The most powerful warrior of the Forever Knights, Connor wanted to destroy the dragon even after he learned the creature's true nature.

KING PATRICK: The Forever Knights are always led by a king. It was Patrick's plan to seek revenge on Ben after he aided the escaped dragon.

THE SQUIRE: Before a man can become a Forever Knight, he must serve as a squire and do the knights' bidding. When the Forever Knights accidentally allowed the dragon to escape, it was the Squire who called in Ben to help.

prisoner was an alien mapmaker who landed on Earth while on an expedition. He longed to return home to be with his family.

Ben reunited the alien with his ship, and he got away. Without a dragon to guard, the knights feared they had lost their purpose. But now they have a new one: to protect Earth from a distant planet of dragons, and to seek revenge on Ben Tennyson and his friends.

THE HIGHBREED

HighBreed aliens seem to be plant-based life-forms. A HighBreed can shoot projectile thorns from its hands as weapons. Roots can sprout from the chest of a thirsty HighBreed to search for water underground. Interestingly, the HighBreed need cold temperatures to survive.

For years, this alien species believed that HighBreed was the only true and pure race in the universe. The HighBreed Supreme Commander ordered that all lesser beings — that is, any being that wasn't pure HighBreed — should be exterminated from the universe.

The HighBreed began to plan the destruction of all other species, planet by planet. They used the same method every time: send a small HighBreed unit to the planet. Transform some of the planet's inhabitants into DNAliens to serve as workers. Build a hyperspace jump gate. Launch a massive surprise attack of warships from across the universe. It was a guaranteed recipe for destruction.

Then the HighBreed came to planet Earth, where Grandpa Max soon discovered their plan. After Max got launched into the Null Void, Ben, Gwen, and Kevin began a quest to find out exactly what the HighBreed were up to.

Ben ended up defeating the HighBreed, but not by destroying them. He used the Omnitrix to find a way to save their dying species from extinction. The HighBreed agreed to leave the rest of the universe in peace.

HiGHBREED HiDEOUT

The HighBreed set up their operation in La Soledad, an abandoned military base. The quartz in the surrounding ground was exactly what they needed to create their jump gate. They used a cloaking device to shield their construction from the outside world. Anyone driving past would see the abandoned buildings of the base, not an alien command center swarming with DNAliens.

THE DNALIENS

The DNAliens are the sinister creations of the HighBreed aliens. To make a DNAlien, you need two ingredients: a slimy parasite called a Xenocite and one helpless human.

The Xenocite latches onto the face of a captured human. The human's DNA is reprogrammed, and the human is transformed into a hideous DNAlien with one huge eyeball and a brain open to the elements.

DNAliens are strong and resistant to attack. While they are equipped with technological weapons, they've got a built-in weapon as well. They shoot out a resinlike goop that quickly hardens. The goop covers victims so they can't move to defend themselves.

You would think that the people of Earth would notice a million one-eyed aliens walking around, but HighBreed technology helps the DNAliens blend into their surroundings. They wear identity masks that make them appear human. Often the masks they wear look like their original human forms.

DNAliens aren't really bad — they're just programmed that way. The HighBreed created them to build a hyperspace jump gate so they could attack Earth.

Ben realized that he could repair the DNAliens with the Omnitrix, returning them to their human forms. In his final battle with the HighBreed, he used up the power in the Omnitrix trying to save DNAliens instead of hurting them. Luckily, Ben's friend Cooper knew about an alien tech device called a Bugzapper. One blast could instantly turn a DNAlien back into a human.

JT AND CASH

JT and Cash have been picking on Ben since second grade. Their bullying used to really bother Ben, but as he got older, he realized it wasn't worth getting upset over.

When Ben finally stood up to JT and Cash — in the parking lot of Mr. Smoothy, his favorite hangout — Cash vowed revenge. He and JT pushed Kevin's car down a hill and stole a large metal glove they found in the trunk. When Cash put on the glove, it slowly transformed him into a superpowerful alien robot.

Cash gave Kevin a pounding and called out Ben for a showdown in the parking lot. Ben didn't want to fight, but had to transform into

ChromaStone when Cash wouldn't back down. They were locked in a dead heat when Ben finally convinced Cash he didn't have to be under the control of his robot body. Cash fought with all his might to become his normal self again. Since then, he and JT have steered clear of Ben and his friends.

D'VOID

Dr. Animo was a re-searcher in veterinary science who once tried to mutate animals in an attempt to take over the world. His evil plans got him sent to the Null Void.

Since he couldn't take over Earth, Dr. Animo tried to take over the Null Void instead. He gained control of the animal-like Null Guardians and began terrorizing the innocent inhabitants of the void. He forced them to mine for Ko-rmite, a powerful stone that he planned to use to break through the impenetrable void. The Kormite also gave him increased power, turning him into the villain known as D'Void.

But D'Void didn't count on Ben finding him in the Null Void. With the help of Grand-pa Max and Plumbers' Help-ers Manny, Helen, and Pierce, Ben destroyed the Kormite furnace — along with Dr. Ani-mo's hopes of domination.

VULKANUS

A Detrovite alien, Vulkanus is a dealer in alien tech weapons. Years ago, he had big plans involving big weapons. But after a few encounters with Ben, he ended up in the Null Void.

Vulkanus escaped and landed back on Earth, where he was stuck swapping Level 3 technology in a dilapidated junkyard. He commanded a small army of underground-dwelling aliens with pickaxes. But Vulkanus wanted more — much more. He captured Kevin and forced him to transform his entire body into a precious gem, Taydenite. He planned to have his minions chip away at Kevin's body bit by bit — until Ben and Gwen showed up to stop him.

Vulkanus looks like a tall, heavily muscled beast wearing thick armor. But during his battle with Ben and Gwen, his lower body shattered, revealing a tiny body supporting Vulkanus's big head. It turns out that this bad guy's tough-looking body was just a robotic shell.

ARGIT

This porcupinelike alien is a tech runner. He arranges deals between criminals who've stolen illegal alien weapons and other criminals who will pay huge sums of money for those weapons.

Argit might not be big or strong, but he's sharp. He can shoot out the piercing quills on his back. They're packed with a poison that paralyzes his victims.

Argit has no loyalty or morals; he's so low, he'd steal food from a hungry rat. Kevin learned this the hard way. He tried to make a deal with Argit by trading Grandpa Max's Rustbucket II. Argit took the Rustbucket and left Kevin with nothing. Ouch! That hurt more than a jab from one of Argit's quills.

MIKE MORNINGSTAR

With his blond hair and piercing blue eyes, this handsome hunk looks like a movie star. When Ben first met Mike, he thought Mike was another hero like him. Ben and his friends were struggling to save bystanders from a collapsed bridge when Mike flew in, trailing glittery stars behind him. When Ben saw Mike's Plumber's badge, he was sure Mike was just the person they needed to join their team and save the world.

Mike was the son of a Plumber, and he had amazing powers — but he was no hero. Mike craved power, and the only way he could get it was by draining the energy of unsuspecting teenage girls, turning them into zombies. When he witnessed Gwen's amazing abilities, he quickly turned on the charm. He knew her strong energy would give him all of the power he wanted.

Mike turned Gwen into a zombie, but she didn't stay that way for long. Gwen fought back and took back her energy. Then the zombie girls got their life force back too. Mike turned into a zombie himself — but that wasn't the end of Mike Morningstar. . . .

DARKSTAR

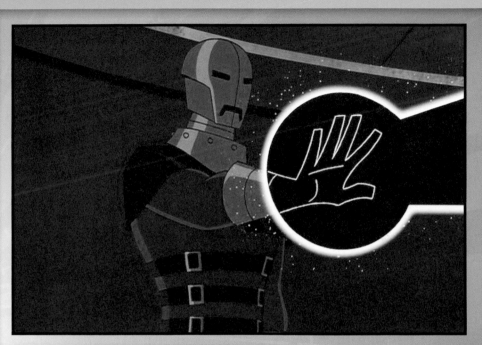

Shriveled and weak, Mike Morningstar vowed revenge on Ben and his friends. He donned a mask, put on a new costume, and became the villain Darkstar.

Darkstar was clever. Knowing he was too weak to fight right away, he tried to get Ben, Gwen, and Kevin sent to the Null Void by framing them for a crime. When all three were about to be arrested by Plumber Magister Gilhil, Darkstar swept in and quickly used his Indigo Beams to drain everyone of their power — everyone except Gwen. She gathered a bunch of angry DNAliens with a grudge against Darkstar to join the fight. They defeated Darkstar, and Gilhil took the villain to the Null Void.

Even though Darkstar was a bad guy, Ben knew he needed all of the Plumbers' kids to help when the HighBreed were poised to destroy Earth. So Gwen and Kevin sprang Darkstar from the Null Void. Darkstar came through — but he disappeared before he could be sent back to the Null Void again.

SEVENSEVEN

SevenSeven is a bounty hunter from the planet Sotoragg. Under his armor is a creature with a large, gaping mouth filled with sharp teeth.

Five years ago, Ben encountered a Sotoraggian bounty hunter named SixSix. He first learned about SevenSeven when he kidnapped Princess Attea of the Incursean Empire. Raff, the right-hand man of the empire, told Ben that SevenSeven was the same race as SixSix, but far more dangerous. "Yeah, eleven more dangerous," Gwen deadpanned.

SevenSeven tried to help Princess Attea overthrow her father's throne, but Swampfire stopped him. SevenSeven's armor cracked, he got one whiff of Swampfire, and then he ran off to wherever it is that bounty hunters hang out.

LORD EMPEROR MILLEUS AND PRINCESS ATTEA

All hail Lord Emperor Milleus, Destroyer of Galaxies! This cruel froglike alien is the leader of the Incursean Empire. With his powerful Conquest Ray and legions of Incursean Warriors, he brings destruction to planets all over the universe.

Milleus was almost responsible for the annihilation of Earth. Bounty hunter Seven-Seven kidnapped his daughter, Princess Attea, and took her to Earth to hide out. Ben and his friends saved the planet in the nick of time.

The emperor's daughter is far from a helpless little princess. After SevenSeven kidnapped her, she made a deal with the bounty hunter: If he helped her overthrow her father, she would pay him double the ransom money. Attea's plan didn't work, and her father sent her to prison for safekeeping until she's truly ready to rule the Incursean Empire.

ALBEDO

Albedo looks like a white-haired Ben Tennyson — but he's an alien trapped in a human body. In his true form he's a Galvan, a small gray creature with yellow bulging eyes and slimy skin.

Albedo was the assistant to Azmuth, the creator of Ben's Omnitrix. He built an inferior copy of the Omnitrix that left him unable to change back into his original body. He traveled to Earth to find Ben in hopes of tricking him into giving him the original Omnitrix.

When Azmuth caught up with his rogue assistant, he administered a unique punishment: Albedo would have to stay in the form of a human teenager for the rest of his life. For Albedo, it's the worst possible future — complete with zits, body odor, and a never-ending craving for chili-cheese fries.

SIMIAN

Simian is the same alien species as Ben's form Spidermonkey: an Arachna-Paniscus. This life-form is native to the planet Arachna. But while Spider-monkey and Simian may look alike, they're very different. One's a hero and the other is a four-armed bandit.

When Ben first met Simian, the thief told him that he was a prince seeking to regain his throne on Arachna. To do that, he needed to return a crystal that had been wielded by his father, the hero King Azuma. Ben and his friends agreed to help retrieve the crystal from a fortress on the moon.

Luckily, Ben figured out Simian's true nature just in time. It turned out that the crystal powered an interga-lactic communications center. Without the crystal, no one would be able to call for help when the DNAliens invaded Earth. Simian was trying to steal the crystal for the High-Breed — but thanks to Ben, he failed.

VILGAX

Vilgax is a Chimera Sui Generis from the Shadow Realm. Ben first encountered this vicious alien warlord when he was ten years old. Vilgax waged a war against Ben in an attempt to gain the Omnitrix for himself. After many battles, Ben finally defeated Vilgax by transforming into Waybig, a superstrong alien who's about a hundred feet tall. He sent Vilgax hurtling into the far reaches of space.

Vilgax made the most of his defeat, conquering new planets and gaining new strength. After five years, he returned to Earth to seek his revenge on Ben. Ben needed to use every trick he knew to defeat Vilgax — but with the Omnitrix broken, it wasn't easy.

In the end, Ben won, and in keeping with the rules of the Galactic Code, Vilgax promised not to return to Earth again. But if Ben ever leaves Earth, Vilgax will be there, ready to seek vengeance once more.

GREATEST FEATS

When your week includes teleporting to the moon, saving Earth from destruction, and communicating with a dragon, you can't say life is boring. Ben and his friends have experienced some really incredible things.

So what's the most exciting moment they've ever experienced? It's hard to choose just one. In this section, you'll learn about the most incredible, unbelievable, unforgettable adventures that Ben, Gwen, and Kevin have had.

BEN'S BEST

Ben's best qualities — his good heart, sharp mind, and ability to connect with the aliens he becomes — have led to some of his most memorable moments.

Ben vs . . . Ben?

What do you do when you're facing a villain with the exact same powers as yours? That's the problem Ben faced when he fought Albedo, a Galvan scientist. Albedo made a copy of the Omnitrix, but it didn't allow him to change back to his original form. He wanted Ben's Omnitrix, and he didn't care how he got it.

Albedo trapped Gwen and Kevin in hard, sticky foam. Then he attacked Ben. Ben transformed into Goop to avoid the foam and aimed an acid blast at Albedo. Albedo turned into Humungousaur and tried to stomp on Goop. Ben countered by turning into Swampfire. He shot mud into Humungousaur's eyes, temporarily blinding him. Then he blasted him with fireballs.

Albedo transformed into Big Chill to put out the flames. The fight raged on. Ben turned into Brain Storm, who fought Big Chill. Albedo as Echo Echo fought Ben as Jet Ray. Albedo became Spidermonkey, but he couldn't trip up Ben's ChromaStone.

In the end, Ben and Albedo were locked in combat in their human forms. The energy from both Omnitrixes was pulling them together. The energy turned Albedo Ben's hair

white and changed the color of his clothes so that he looked like Ben's opposite.

The fight ended when Azmuth transported in and broke the energy field between the two devices. You could say the battle ended in a tie. But if he ever escapes from the prison of his human body, you can be sure Albedo will be back to try to defeat Ben once and for all.

The Dragon Speaks

With their massive size, fiery breath, and leathery wings, dragons are some of the most well-known creatures in mythology. Nobody could guess that there was a connection between dragons and aliens — nobody except Ben Tennyson.

The Forever Knights kept a dragon captive for a thousand years. When it escaped, they called Ben to help them capture it. When Ben got close to the creature, he became convinced it was trying to

tell him something. Then he saw what looked like
a broken translator box on the dragon's neck.
Instead of blasting it, Ben decided to
give the dragon a chance to speak.

How do you get close enough to an
angry dragon to replace its translator box?
Ben used Spidermonkey for the job. He
jumped on the dragon's neck, but was
quickly thrown off.

Before he could hit the ground,
Spidermonkey threw out a web
and attached it to a ceiling beam.
The dragon hurled heat blast after
heat blast at Spidermonkey, but he
dodged them all. Gwen sent out a
force field to protect him, and Spidermonkey
wrapped the dragon in his webbing. Then he
quickly jumped up and replaced the broken translator box with a new one.

Instantly, the dragon's roars turned into
speech. Ben learned that he was an alien from a
distant planet, and he helped the dragon return
home to his family.

The Power of Friendship

While locked in a battle with a HighBreed, Ben and the alien were accidentally transported to a barren planet, Turrawaste. They had a day's journey to the teleporter pod ahead of them, and the path was marked with dangerous, predatory beasts.

The HighBreed, Reinrassig III, wanted nothing to do with a lowly life-form like Ben. But Ben knew they would have to work together to survive the

journey. He never gave up trying to get through to "Reiny." When the HighBreed suffered from the intense heat, Ben cooled him down with Big Chill. When the HighBreed lost his arm saving Ben from a dangerous creature, Ben used Swampfire's vines to reattach it.

It seemed like all of Ben's efforts were for nothing. When they reached the transporter pod, Reiny refused to go, saying he was contaminated. But in the end, it was Reiny who convinced the High-Breed Supreme Commander that the HighBreed could live in harmony with other species. Ben's small acts of kindness had one huge result: They helped save the world.

GWEN'S BEST

She's able to deflect laser blasts, walk on air, and kick monster butt — all thanks to her glowing pink energy.

Girl Power

Nobody can blame Gwen for being charmed by Mike Morningstar. After all, he flew down from the sky to save a girl in trouble. Plus he had perfect blond hair and blue eyes, and left a glittery trail of stardust behind him when he flew.

Mike told Gwen, Ben, and Kevin that he was the son of a Plumber. He agreed to help them fight the alien invasion. But what he really wanted was Gwen's energy. Mike had already drained the life-force from the girls in his fancy prep school, turning them into zombies. He knew Gwen's energy would give him strength he could scarcely even imagine.

When Mike drained Gwen's energy, it looked as if she would remain a zombie forever. But Gwen tapped into her inner strength. Even though Mike had weakened her, she overcame him and took her power back. Mike Morningstar learned the hard way that messing with Gwen was a bad idea.

Help in Unusual Places

Things were looking grim. The villain Darkstar had tricked a HighBreed alien into helping him capture Kevin and his friends. Only Gwen escaped. Darkstar trapped Ben, Kevin, the HighBreed, and a Plumber, Magister Gilhil. He bound them in chains and had them suspended in midair by a powerful force field.

Gwen knew she couldn't defeat Darkstar alone, so she did some quick thinking. She knew that the DNAliens were loyal to their HighBreed commander. She took a chance and asked them to help her. They could have attacked Gwen, but instead they launched an assault on Darkstar.

When the force field dissipated, Kevin transformed into steel and freed Ben and Magister Gilhil. Thanks to Gwen, Darkstar was captured and sent into the Null Void.

So...Much...Power

Earth was moments away from being destroyed. Fleets of HighBreed warships were poised to travel through the hyperspace jump gate. Ben, Gwen, and Kevin raced to the HighBreed command center to try to get the HighBreed to close the gate.

They faced off against the HighBreed Earth Commander and two other HighBreed. Ben fought the commander as Swampfire. Kevin turned into stone and attacked one of the HighBreed. The powerful alien pounded Kevin into the floor, shattering his stone shell. Then the HighBreed faced Gwen.

"Perhaps I'll finish your friend first, so you can watch him suffer."

A strange feeling came over Gwen. Her entire body transformed into a being of pure pink energy. Somehow she had become a full Anodite alien, just like her grandmother.

One blast of Anodite energy took care of the HighBreed. Gwen felt the strength rising in her. She felt like she could take down the entire HighBreed fleet. But was she prepared to pay the cost?

Kevin knew that if she stayed in her Anodite form, she would lose her humanity completely. He begged her to come back. Gwen controlled the powerful energy inside her and returned to her human form.

KEVIN'S BEST

He's the man of steel— and stone, and chrome, and wood, and whatever else he can touch.

Kevin vs Mike Morningstar

When Mike Morningstar arrived on the scene like a shining star, Ben and Gwen were happy to meet him. Ben was eager to recruit Plumbers' kids like Mike to join their team. And Gwen fell under Mike's charming spell.

Only Kevin was suspicious of Mike. He figured out that Mike was draining girls of their energy, and he and Ben raced to Gwen's rescue. When he saw that Mike had already turned Gwen into a zombie, he transformed into concrete. Concrete Kevin charged up the stairs and tackled Mike, sending them both crashing to the ground below. Mike used an energy blast to toss Kevin off of him, but Kevin's move gave Gwen time to find the strength she needed to get her power back from the deceitful villain.

Rubber Kevin

Things were looking grim for Earth. Lord Emperor Milleus had ordered his lackey, Raff, to destroy the planet with the powerful Conquest Ray. Raff held the detonator in his hands, ready to press the button.

Then . . . bounce! Kevin transformed into rubber and knocked Raff down, grabbing the detonator. Raff sent Incursean warriors in pursuit, and Kevin took them down like bowling pins. Rubber Kevin might not be as strong as Stone Kevin or Steel Kevin, but he's got some pretty mean moves!

A Good Guy After All

Ben and Gwen were happy when Kevin joined their alien-fighting team. But he wasn't on the team long before he stole Grandpa Max's Rustbucket II!

Things didn't look good for Kevin. He was hoping to trade the Rustbucket II for an alien tech device from a dealer called Vulkanus. But he got double-crossed by Argit, an alien tech runner. Ben and Gwen were sure Kevin was back to his old thieving ways.

But Kevin surprised them both. Ben and Gwen soon learned that the alien tech device he was trying to get was a holo-viewer that contained a special message from Grandpa Max. Kevin was just using some old connections to help the team. After that, Ben and Gwen knew they could trust Kevin, no matter what.

GLOSSARY

ANODITE: A being from the planet Anodyne. Anodites can manipulate living energy and are able to become pure energy beings.

BUGZAPPER: A device used to turn DNAliens back into humans.

DASYPODIDAE: This creature from the planet Turrawuste may be small, but it can mean big trouble. Dasypodidae attack in swarms and, like piranhas on Earth, they will tear apart prey in a furious feeding frenzy.

DRAVEC: This alien monster looks like a giant worm with a mouthful of sharp teeth. It lives under the sand and emerges to surprise its prey. It is native to the planet Turrawuste.

GALVAN PRIME: A scientifically advanced world. It is home to the scientist Azmuth, who created the Omnitrix.

HOLO-VIEWER: A small device capable of projecting a three-dimensional holographic image of the person sending a message.

HYPERSPACE JUMP GATE:
A device capable of opening up huge rifts in hyperspace that allow large warships to cross the galaxy in a matter of seconds.

KORMITE:
A glowing rock found in the Null Void. It is a powerful fuel source.

MAGISTER:
A rank in the Plumbers. A magister is in charge of other Plumbers in several space quadrants.

MANNA:
The life energy found in everything from aliens to humans to plants. Gwen can use Manna to track down a living thing by following its energy trail.

MR. SMOOTHY:
This fast-food joint is where Ben gets his favorite drink — smoothies. Ben is happy to slurp down turnips and wheatgrass juice mixed with ginger, but Kevin won't go near the healthy drinks.

NULL GUARDS:
Created by the Galvans, these creatures are the faceless watchdogs of the Null Void. Their job is to keep inhabitants of the Null Void safe from the dangerous criminals there.

NULL VOID: An extradimensional prison for intergalactic criminals. It's where the Plumbers send the bad guys they catch. But not everyone in the Null Void is evil. The Null Void was originally created by the Galvans as a penal colony. Over time, communities of families sprang up there. Then other species started using the Null Void as a criminal dumping ground.

NULL VOID PROJECTOR: Plumbers use this handheld device, which shoots out a beam. Whatever the beam hits gets sent directly into the Null Void.

PLUMBERS: Members of an inter-galactic police force.

PLUMBERS' BADGES: Round, glowing badges carried by Plumbers. The badges can be used to track the location of other Plumbers and send distress signals to other badges. Each badge contains a translation circuit that automatically translates alien language into the Plumber's native language. Ben's Omnitrix contains many of the same features as a Plumbers' badge.

PLUMBERS' SNAKE: An unbreakable pan-dimensional retrieval system. It's basically a long cable you can attach to something before sending it into the inescapable Null Void. To retrieve whatever you've sent in, just reel in the cable.

TAYDENITE: The rarest, most precious gem in the galaxy.

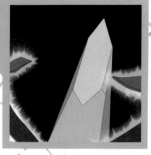

TECHNOPATH: Someone who is able to communicate with technology. Ben's friend Cooper is a technopath.

TELEPORTER POD: Who needs a flying saucer for space travel when you've got a teleporter pod? Step inside this handy device and you can be transported to one of the many pods located all over the universe.

TURRAWUSTE: A desert planet. There's not much happening on Turrawuste. Its main use is as a relay station for intergalactic transport.

WRENCH: When Grandpa Max ended up in the Null Void, he found that the evil Dr. Animo had become the superpowerful D'Void, and taken control of the extradimensional prison world. Grandpa Max took on the identity of the Wrench and led the fight against D'Void.

XENOCITE: A slimy parasite that looks half lobster, half larvae. When it latches onto a human's face, the doomed human is transformed into a DNAlien.

WHAT'S YOUR INNER 10?

Which of Ben's alien forms are you most like? Take these two quizzes to find out.

QUIZ #1

1. What is your biggest strength?
a. Your ability to adapt to any situation
b. Your agility and speed
c. Your intelligence
d. Your strength
e. The stench under your armpits

2. Which of these colors do you like best?
a. Bright green
b. Blue
c. Gray
d. Brown
e. Forest green

3. Which of these things found in nature is your favorite?
a. The slimy trail left by a slug
b. Bananas
c. Lightning storms
d. Mountains
e. Plants

4. You are walking down a trail and a big rock blocks your path. What do you do?
a. Slide under it
b. Jump over it
c. Devise a complicated lever to remove it
d. Stomp on it
e. Dig a tunnel in the mud underneath it

5. What do you look for in a planet?
a. Intense heat and oozing lava
b. Tall trees with lots of vines
c. Other intelligent beings to converse with
d. Lots of open space
e. Nice wet marshes

WHICH ALIEN ARE YOU MOST LIKE?

If you answered mostly a's,
then you're like Goop.
You fit in almost anywhere,
but people feel a little
uncomfortable around you.

If you answered mostly b's,
then you're like Spidermonkey.
You might want to consider
joining a sports team because
you can really move!

If you answered mostly c's,
then you're like Brain Storm.
But of course, you're so smart,
you knew that already.

If you answered mostly d's,
then you're like Humungousaur.
You're probably due for a
big growth spurt soon.

If you answered mostly e's,
then you're like Swampfire.
You might want to invest
in some deodorant.

QUIZ #2

1. What's your favorite food?
   a. Water
   b. You don't need food — you are one with the universe.
   c. Crunchy cereal
   d. An all-you-can-eat buffet. You've got a lot of mouths to feed.
   e. Ice cream

2. What do you like to do in your spare time?
   a. Go swimming
   b. Gaze at the stars
   c. Go rock climbing
   d. Listen to music
   e. Watch a scary movie

3. Which of these would you say is your best physical feature?
   a. Your extra-long arms
   b. Your beautiful mind
   c. Your massive shoulders
   d. Your big mouth
   e. Your haunting eyes

4. What's your favorite sound?
   a. The sound of waves washing up on the shore
   b. The sound of silence
   c. Rock and roll
   d. The sound of your own voice
   e. The sound of people gasping in terror when they see you

5. If you could live in one of these places, which would you choose?
   a. A lake
   b. The vastness of space
   c. A cave
   d. The Grand Canyon
   e. The North Pole

WHICH ALIEN ARE YOU MOST LIKE?

If you answered mostly a's,
you are like Jet Ray.
You're only happy when it rains.

If you answered mostly b's,
you're like Alien X.
You don't like being around
people that much.

If you answered mostly c's,
you're like ChromaStone.
You may have a hard head,
but you're not hard to like!

If you answered mostly d's,
you're like Echo Echo.
There's more of you to love!

If you answered mostly e's,
you're like Big Chill. You
always keep your cool.